Little Turtle
Gets Lost

4/100

by Jean Gnap
Illustrations by J.P. Roberts

To Abigail,
Home is the best place and perhaps the safest!

Jean Gnap

From Grammy and Pee Paw

In a small town not too far away, on a tree-lined street, there was a charming brown brick house. It had a huge grassy backyard, a tall evergreen on the front lawn, a big front porch, and a lost little turtle sitting on the first step.

Little Turtle was trying to climb the stairs to the front porch, but he kept falling back onto the first step.

Robins screeched, "Help the turtle! Help the turtle! A hawk is circling and may swoop down and eat him!"

As they raced back and forth, climbed trees, and jumped from branch to branch, squirrels chattered, "Get help! Get help! A hawk is circling!"

Little Turtle kept struggling to get up the stairs, but his legs were too short to reach. On the last try, he tumbled onto his back and could not right himself. He rocked back and forth, waving his little feet in the air. I am in trouble, he thought. Why did I leave the lake?

The ruckus brought 12-year-old Matt out of the house. Barefoot, freckled, brown-haired Matt skipped down the stairs and said, "What is going on out here?"

His younger brother, Mike, came to the door and peeked out.

The robins stopped screeching. The squirrels stopped chattering. Little Turtle did not move a muscle. But the hawk kept circling!

Matt noticed Little Turtle upside down on the first step. "What in the world are you doing out of the lake?" asked Matt.

Of course Little Turtle did not answer. He was as still as a rock!

The hawk saw Matt and decided to look for dinner somewhere else. The robins were relieved. The squirrels were relieved. Little Turtle was especially relieved.

"How did you get here?" asked Matt as he picked up Little Turtle. The lake was two blocks away, across a busy street.

"I went exploring, but then I got lost. Instead of going back to the lake, I took a wrong turn," said Little Turtle. "I saw children playing in a nearby park and hoped that they would take me back to the lake, but I had to cross a very busy street. By the time I dodged all the cars and trucks and got across the street, the children were gone. Then I saw this house, so I tried to get up the stairs and find help."

Of course, Matt could not hear Little Turtle speaking. Boys could not hear "turtle talk." But the robins and squirrels could hear Little Turtle as plain as day. "Whatever made you go exploring?" they asked.

"Actually, I was looking for someplace quiet to live," said Little Turtle. "The lake is so noisy, both day and night. Frogs are croaking, fish flopping, mosquitos humming, bees buzzing, dragonflies zooming, and ducks quacking. I can even hear the lily pad flowers open and close each day."

Matt could not hear the animals talking to one another. They talked on "animal wavelength," so humans could not hear them. But the evergreen could. He offered some advice.

"Maybe Matt will return Little Turtle to the lake," said the evergreen. "But what will Little Turtle do then? I think he should have earplugs. Yes, that is what he needs—earplugs!"

"That is strange advice," said the robins and the squirrels. "We don't see any ears on Little Turtle, do you?"

"Actually, no, I do not. But maybe his ears are hidden," said the evergreen. "Yes, that is it! His ears have to be hidden. How else could he hear all that noise at the lake?"

In the meantime, Matt brought out a big bowl filled with water and put Little Turtle in it.

"You need to be in some water. It's hot out today, and you were probably traveling for a long time," said Matt. "I don't want you to get sick. I'll take you back to the lake in a little while."

"Oh no!" said Little Turtle. "The lake is too noisy. I was trying to find a new home. But I got lost and did not know where I was or how to get back to the lake."

But of course, Matt could not hear Little Turtle speaking. Boys could not hear "turtle talk."

"You're in a fine fix," said the robins.

"Did you even think about what you were going to eat?" asked the squirrels.

"Did you even think about where you were going to live? You can't live in a tree," said the evergreen.

"You need an area with water," they all chided Little Turtle. "Puddles dry up after a rain, so you can't live in a puddle. You can't live in a sewer because it is too dirty there. All the other lakes will be noisy, too. What were you thinking?"

A few tears fell into the bowl of water, and Little Turtle sniffled.

"I just do not know what to do. I guess I was not planning very well," said Little Turtle. "In fact, I could have been smashed by a big truck when I was crossing the street. Come to think of it, maybe that is why the cars and trucks were weaving back and forth as they were driving past me."

"You could have caused an accident. You were lucky, and so were the cars and trucks," said the evergreen.

A great big tear dropped into the water. Kerplunk!

Matt came out of the house with a plastic bag and dumped Little Turtle and the water into it. He zipped it closed and put it into his backpack. Then he got onto his bike. Away he peddled to the lake.

The robins and squirrels sighed, "Well, that is a relief. Little Turtle will be taken back to his home. But what about the noise? What will he do about the noise?

At the lake, Matt parked his bike, opened his backpack, took out the plastic bag, and released Little Turtle into the water.

"Well, you are safe again," said Matt. He got back on his bike and started for home.

Little Turtle sadly said, "Thank you."

But of course, Matt could not hear him. Boys could not hear "turtle talk."

The lake was very active. Fish were flopping, bees buzzing, ducks quacking, and dragonflies zooming. Soon mosquitos would be humming, frogs croaking, and lily pads closing. Fortunately, the hawk was nowhere to be seen.

Little Turtle did not look happy as he swam toward a half-submerged log and climbed onto it. Other turtles were sunning themselves on it.

"Welcome back," they said. "Where were you?"

"I was on an adventure," said Little Turtle. "I was exploring."

"Is that so? You are lucky that you were not run over by a big truck and flattened like a pancake," they laughed.

Little Turtle was humiliated and vowed to think of a better plan to find a new home.

Many days and nights went by. Little Turtle could not think of anything.

One day Matt came to the lake to fish. As he sat on the bank watching his bobber get a bite, he said, "This lake is such a beautiful site." He sighed happily.

"The water is so clean and clear that you can see the bottom. Little fish dart back and forth under the lily pads, and that blue heron looks so stately on the rock near the waterfall. Turtles are sunning themselves on logs, and there are lots of bees, butterflies, and dragonflies. Fish jump and splash. Trees and beautiful flowers surround the lake, and people can walk, bike the trails, and canoe." Matt looked around again. "What a wonderful place—peaceful, welcoming, beautiful!"

Little Turtle heard all of that and started to think.

"This lake is a beautiful place, and it is not really that noisy. The sounds are the sounds of nature," said Little Turtle. "I did not take the time to look about and see the wonderful plants and animals. They are my friends and family. This is my home. Shame on me for not appreciating my lake."

Matt reeled in his fishing rod, got on his bike, and started for home. But as he left, he was absolutely sure that he heard a small voice drifting from a nearby log.

The voice said, "Thank you, lake, for frogs croaking, fish flopping, mosquitos humming, bees buzzing, dragonflies zooming, ducks quacking, and turtles sunning. Thank you, lake, for trails, flowers, and trees. Thank you, lake, for being my home!"

Lo and behold, gently floating along the surface of the water on a soft breeze, another voice said, "you are welcome!"

The End

Acknowledgments

This book is dedicated to Mayor Eugene Simpson, his vision, and to all the staff and volunteers who help at the lake. For sure the lake is home to all the people who love the lake.
Often called the "JEWEL" of the small town, the lake celebrated it's 25th anniversary during 2016. Come visit!

Recently Published

The Puppy Who Wanted To Be A Boy
-*Accept who you are, but be the best that you can be.*

Will Old Rusty Ever Get To Go To The Classic Car Show?
-*Dreams Fulfilled?*

Future Stories

Baby Robin Won't Eat Worms
-*It's okay to be different.*

The Secret Adventures of Flutter And Flitter
-*While on a secret adventure a Monarch Butterfly and a Hine's Emerald Dragonfly help the cause of endangered species. But is their secret adventure really secret?*

Will Little Fir Tree Become A Real Christmas Tree?
-*Mother Nature steps in with magic!*

The Fat Little Duck Who Could Not Fly
-*Best to listen to good advice.*

Uh-Oh! Little Field Mouse Goes To Story Hour
-*The Library gets a most unusual guest!*

Sing To The Sun
-*A song of appreciation with a surprise ending.*